I CALL MY HAND GENTLE

STORY BY AMANDA HAAN
PICTURES BY MARINA SAGONA

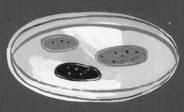

viking

VIKING
Published by the Penguin Group
Penguin Putnam Books for Young Readers,
345 Hudson Street, New York, New York 10014, U.S.A.
Penguin Books Ltd, 80 Strand, London WC2R ORL, England
Penguin Books Australia Ltd, Ringwood, Victoria, Australia
Penguin Books Canada Ltd, 10 Alcorn Avenue, Toronto, Ontario, Canada M4V 3B2
Penguin Books (N.Z.) Ltd, 182-190 Wairau Road, Auckland 10, New Zealand

Penguin Books Ltd, Registered Offices: Harmondsworth, Middlesex, England

First published in 2003 by Viking, a division of Penguin Putnam Books for Young Readers.

3 5 7 9 10 8 6 4

Text copyright © Amanda Haan, 2003
Illustrations copyright © Marina Sagona, 2003

LIBRARY OF CONGRESS CATALOGING-IN-PUBLICATION DATA
Haan, Amanda.
I call my hand gentle / story by Amanda Haan ; pictures by Marina Sagona.
p.   cm.
Summary: A girl describes how her hands are special and how she chooses
to have them do productive and gentle things.
ISBN 0-670-03621-8 (hardcover)
[1. Hand—Fiction. 2. Choice—Fiction.] I. Sagona, Marina, ill. II. Title.
PZ7.H111315 Ic 2003   [E]—dc21   2002012697

Manufactured in China
Book design by Marina Sagona
Typography by Teresa Kietlinski
Set in Journal

FOR STEVE, KATE,
MY FAMILY, & TORINO
—A.H.

FOR ANNA & VIOLA
—M.S.

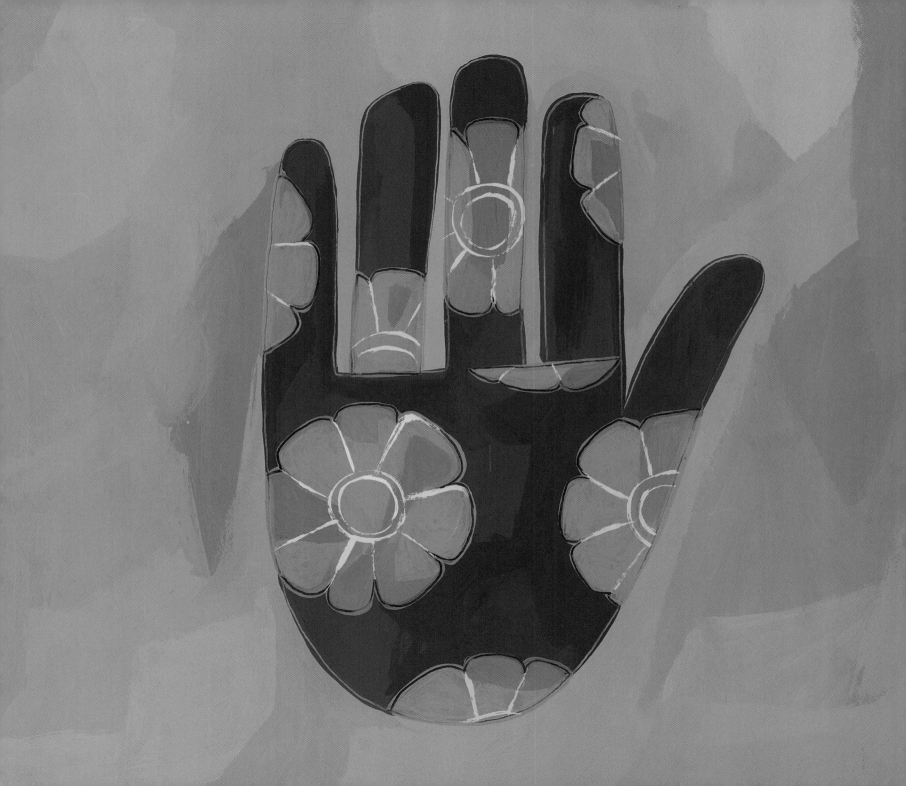

THIS
IS
MY
HAND

IT CAN HUG

THROW

IT CAN HOLD

IT CAN PROTECT

WHAT DO I KNOW

ABOUT MY HAND?

IT
CAN'T DO
THINGS
WITHOUT
ME

IT DOES
WHAT
I WANT
IT TO
DO

WHEN I WANT TO PLAY,

IT CAN CATCH,

BUILD,

& HIDE

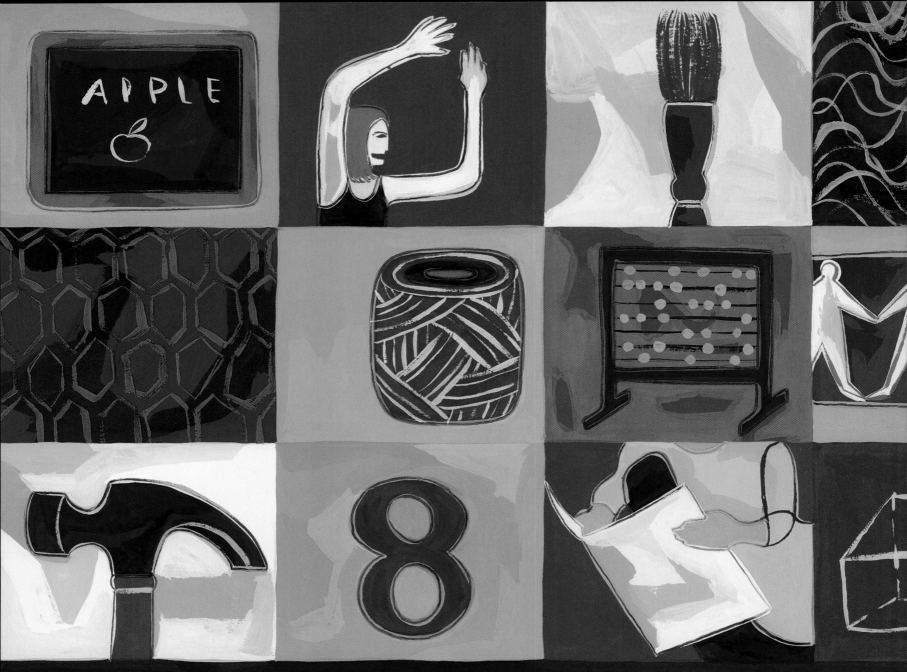

WHEN I WANT TO WORK, IT

CAN HAMMER, WRITE, & COUNT

ALL OF THESE THINGS
I CHOOSE,

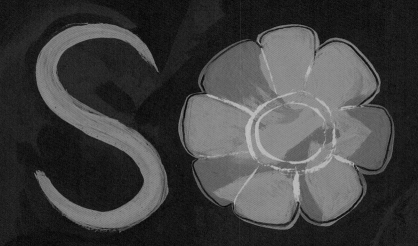

S❀

I CHOOSE NOT TO...

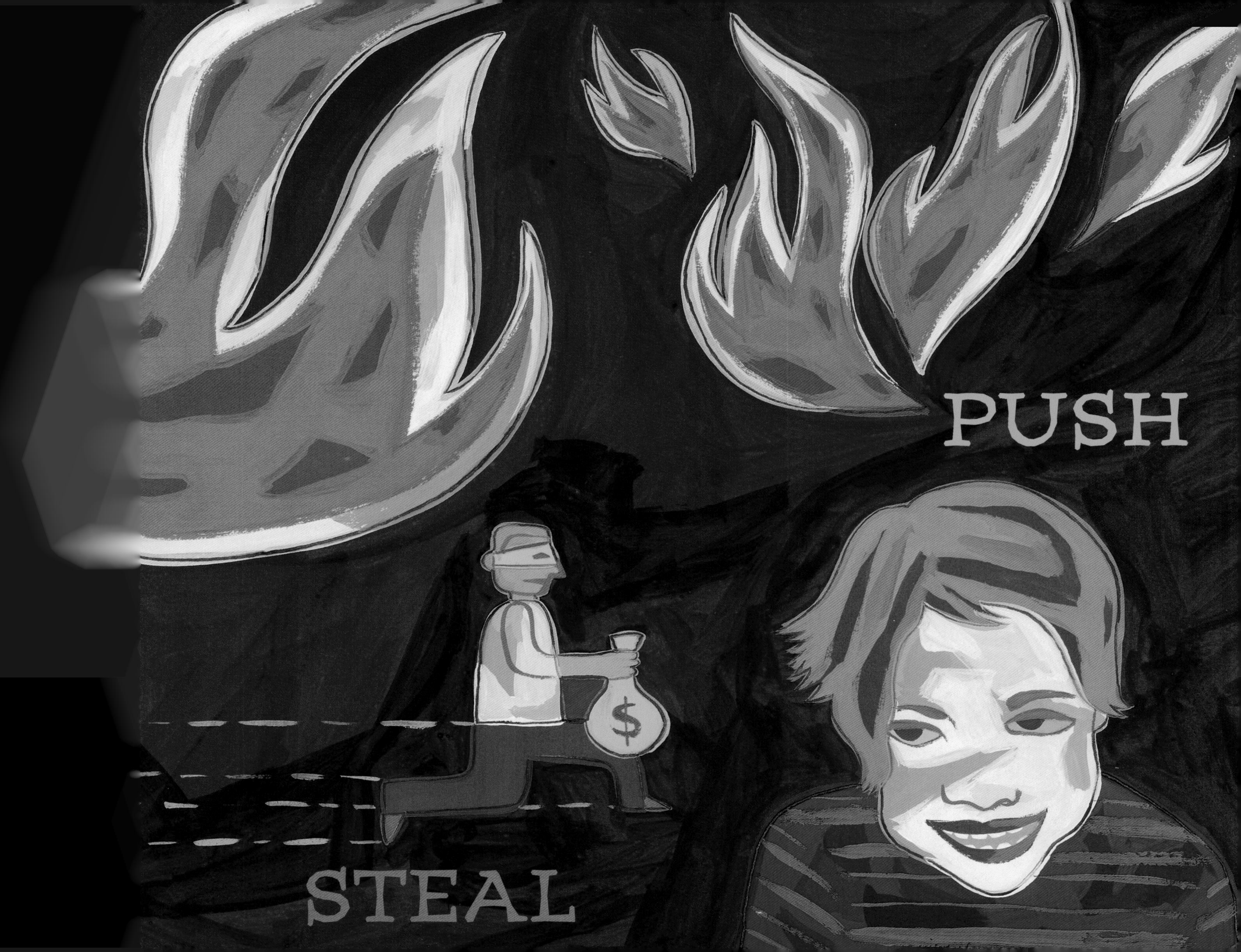
PUSH
STEAL

HURT

GRAB

OR BREAK

I LIKE TO PET CUDDLE

TICKLE & SHARE WITH MY HANDS

SO I'LL CALL
MY HAND
GENTLE

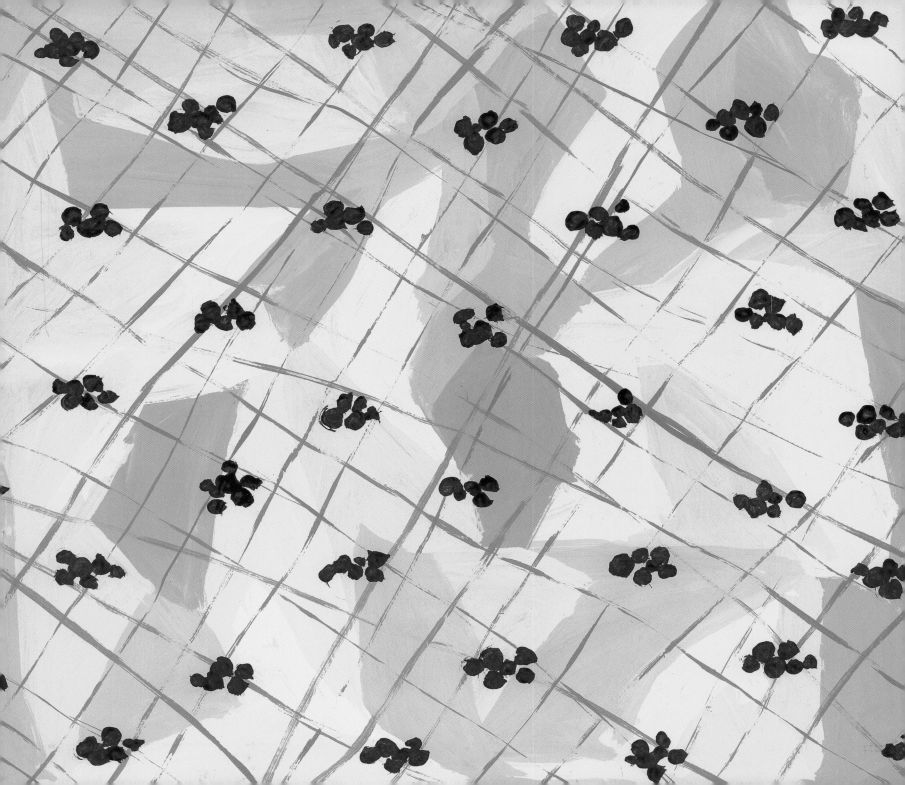